MEET THE CHARACTERS

BEN TENNYSON
TEN TIMES MORE TROUBLE THAN THE AVERAGE KID!

GWEN TENNYSON
RED-HEADED VOICE OF REASON TO HER COUSIN BEN

GRANDPA MAX
JUST A MILD-MANNERED GRANDFATHER - OR IS HE?...

VILGAX
ALIEN WARLORD WITH A REAL ATTITUDE PROBLEM

FOUR ARMS
PROOF THAT FOUR ARMS ARE BETTER THAN TWO

HEATBLAST
THIS ALIEN'S ON FIRE!

STINKFLY
THERE'S NO FLY SWAT BIG ENOUGH FOR THIS INSECT

DIAMONDHEAD
YOU COULD SAY HE'S A SHARP SHOOTER

UPGRADE
NEVER HAS A PROBLEM WTH MODERN TECHNOLOGY...

GHOSTFREAK
YOU WON'T FIND HIM BEATING HIS HEAD AGAINST BRICK WALLS

GREY MATTER
HE'S A CLEVER LITTLE THING

WILDMUTT
HE'S ONE DOGGIE YOU SHOULDN'T PET!

RIPJAWS
NEVER BITES OFF MORE THAN HE CAN CHEW

XLR8
HE'S ALWAYS UP TO SPEED

EGMONT
We bring stories to life

First published in Great Britain 2010 by Dean,
an imprint of Egmont UK Limited,
239 Kensington High Street, London W8 6SA
All Rights Reserved

ISBN 978 0 6035 6516 8
3 5 7 9 10 8 6 4 2
Printed and bound in Italy

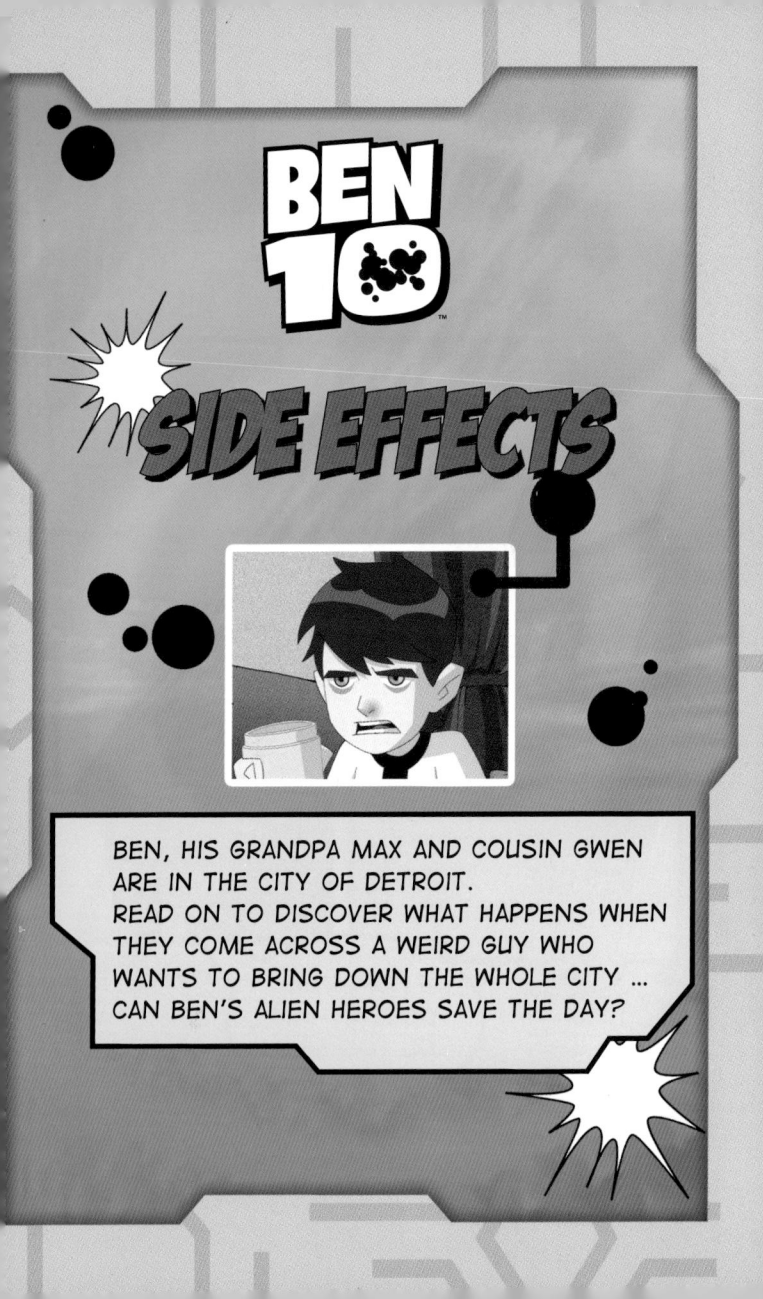

BEN 10

SIDE EFFECTS

BEN, HIS GRANDPA MAX AND COUSIN GWEN
ARE IN THE CITY OF DETROIT.
READ ON TO DISCOVER WHAT HAPPENS WHEN
THEY COME ACROSS A WEIRD GUY WHO
WANTS TO BRING DOWN THE WHOLE CITY ...
CAN BEN'S ALIEN HEROES SAVE THE DAY?

IT'S DAYTIME, IN DOWNTOWN DETROIT. CONSTRUCTION WORKERS HAVE MOVED IN TO DEMOLISH AN APARTMENT BUILDING.

SUDDENLY, A STRANGE FIGURE APPEARS FROM THE RUBBLE. HIS NAME IS CLANCY.

HE GLARES AT THE WORKERS, HIS NARROW EYES GLOWING. THE MEN BEGIN TO PANIC.

GET OUT OF OUR HOUSE!

CLANCY PULLS OPEN HIS COAT AND A SWARM OF *INSECTS* FLIES OUT, ATTACKING THE WORKERS.

I HOPE THIS DOESN'T BUG YOU TOO MUCH!

MEANWHILE,
IN THE SAME CITY, GRANDPA MAX
AND GWEN ARE MOTORING ALONG IN THE
RUSTBUCKET. THEY'RE FOLLOWING A SPEEDING
GETAWAY CAR. JUST AHEAD OF THEM IS A
SOUPED-UP MOTORBIKE - ONE IMPRESSIVE
UPGRADE MACHINE!

UPGRADE SWERVES
AROUND CARS LEFT
AND RIGHT AS HE
GETS CLOSER TO
THE GETAWAY CAR.

LOOK OUT! ONE SIDE!
COMING THROUGH!

HE FIRES A LASER BEAM AT
THE CAR, BLOWING THE
BOOT OPEN. OUT FLY TWO
HUGE MONEY BAGS.

UPGRADE GETS ALONGSIDE THE CAR. HE POPS
OUT THE BIKE'S KICKSTAND, WHICH WORKS LIKE
A SHARP DRILL BIT TO CUT RIGHT THROUGH TWO
OF THE CAR'S WHEELS. IT CAN'T GO ANYWHERE
WITHOUT WHEELS!

THE CAR SPINS WILDLY AND CRASHES TO A
HALT. THE THIEF INSIDE GROANS AT THE BIKE
WITH NO DRIVER.

WITH THE POLICE ON THEIR WAY, THE UPGRADE MOTORBIKE DRIVES OVER TO A PARKED ICE-CREAM VAN. UPGRADE DISLODGES HIMSELF FROM THE BIKE AND MERGES WITH THE ICE-CREAM VAN, *OOZING* INSIDE OF IT!

WELL, I DID JUST NAB THE BAD GUY ... NOW WE'RE TALKIN'!

GRANDPA MAX AND GWEN ARRIVE. "WHERE'S BEN?" ASKS MAX.

"LONG CHASE, HOT DAY ... I'M THINKING ..." SAYS GWEN, POINTING AT THE ICE-CREAM VAN.

GRANDPA MAX OPENS UP THE ICE-CREAM VAN. INSIDE, THEY FIND UPGRADE SHIVERING, SURROUNDED BY A PILE OF ICE-CREAM WRAPPERS!

SUDDENLY THE OMNITRIX BLEEPS, AND IT'S BEN SITTING THERE, SHIVERING IN THE ICE-CREAM VAN. HE'S CAUGHT A REALLY BAD COLD!

BEEP! BEEP!

WHAT BEN NEEDS IS A DOSE OF MY FAMOUS SANG JU YIN PIAN COLD REMEDY. LET'S GO. CHINATOWN'S JUST DOWN THE ROAD.

IN CHINATOWN, COUNCILWOMAN JOYCE LIANG IS MAKING A SPEECH. "LADIES AND GENTLEMEN, I WANT TO THANK YOU ALL FOR YOUR SUPPORT OF MY RE-DEVELOPMENT PROGRAMME. IT'S TRULY A DREAM COME TRUE," SHE SAYS.

HUMMMMMM

SUDDENLY THERE'S A LOUD HUMMING NOISE, AND A SWARM OF WASPS DESCENDS. IN THE MIDDLE OF THEM IS CLANCY!

YOU'RE NOT TEARING DOWN OUR APARTMENT BUILDING, WE WON'T LET YOU.

YOU'RE THE STRANGE GUY WHO WOULDN'T LEAVE. WHAT ARE YOU DOING?

JUST BRINGING YOU HOME FOR DINNER ... YOU'RE THE MAIN COURSE.

THE WASPS SWARM AROUND JOYCE LIANG, COVERING HER.

BACK IN THE RUSTBUCKET, BEN'S LAID UP. GRANDPA MAX GIVES HIM A GLASS OF HIS DISGUSTING-LOOKING COLD REMEDY.

IT'S PUTRID STUFF.

IT SEEMS YOUR COLD HAS SPREAD TO ALL YOUR ALIENS, AS WELL. THERE'S NO TELLING HOW IT'LL AFFECT THEM.

IT'S NOT JUST YOU I'M WORRIED ABOUT.

GWEN LOOKS UP FROM HER LAPTOP.

"GOT IT! BUG EYES SAID SOMETHING ABOUT KNOCKING DOWN HIS BUILDING. THE ONLY APARTMENT LEFT FOR DEMOLITION IS AT 8610 CHESTER STREET," SAYS GWEN.

GRANDPA MAX GETS BEHIND THE WHEEL OF THE RUSTBUCKET. THE TEAM IS ON ITS WAY!

THE GANG HEAR JOYCE LIANG SCREAM JUST AS FOUR ARMS APPEARS. GRABBING GRANDPA MAX AND GWEN, HE RUNS UPSTAIRS TO LOOK FOR HER!

THE RUSTBUCKET PULLS UP OUTSIDE. GRANDPA MAX AND GWEN TAKE A LOOK AROUND, BEN WANDERS OFF.

OUR GRANDFATHER BUILT THIS BUILDING. WE GREW UP HERE, JUST ME AND MY LITTLE FRIENDS.

AT 8610 CHESTER STREET, INSIDE CLANCY'S APARTMENT, THE COUNCILWOMAN IS TRAPPED. BLACK WIDOW SPIDERS ARE CRAWLING ALL OVER HER.

CLANCY APPEARS BEHIND EVERYONE, WITH AN ARMY OF BEETLES AND COCKROACHES.

YOU ARE TRESPASSING. WE WILL RULE MANKIND!

AT CLANCY'S COMMAND, A SWARM OF MOSQUITOES DIVE BOMBS MAX. HE JUMPS OUT OF THE WAY. GWEN IS CORNERED BY TERMITES THAT ARE EATING THE WOODEN FLOORBOARDS BENEATH HER FEET.

FOUR ARMS IS ATTACKED BY ANTS. HE JUMPS AROUND WILDLY, TRYING TO SHAKE THEM OFF. HE ACCIDENTALLY PUTS HIS LEGS THROUGH WALLS, AND HIS FIST THROUGH THE CEILING.

YOU ARE DESTROYING OUR HOME!

GRANDPA MAX AND JOYCE PULL GWEN TO SAFETY, NARROWLY DODGING THE FALLING DEBRIS.

WHEN THE TEAM ARRIVES AT THE NUCLEAR POWER PLANT, ALARMS ARE RINGING AND LIGHTS ARE FLASHING. THE DOOR TO THE REACTOR'S CONTROL ROOM HAS BEEN SMASHED OPEN AND THE CONTROLS HAVE BEEN DESTROYED.

CORE TEMPERATURE RISING, APPROACHING CRITICAL ...

CORE TEMPERATURE CRITICAL, MELTDOWN IMMINENT ...

CLANCY ENTERS. HE'S WEARING A PROTECTIVE BODYSUIT – A TOUGH, THICK, DISGUSTING SHELL OF COCKROACHES!

COME FOR A FRONT ROW SEAT? WHEN THE REACTOR GOES SUPER-CRITICAL, I'LL BE AS SNUG AS A BUG IN A RUG!

"OF COURSE. SCIENTISTS THINK COCKROACHES ARE THE ONLY THINGS THAT WOULD SURVIVE A NUCLEAR BLAST!" SHOUTS GWEN.

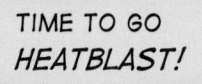

TIME TO GO *HEATBLAST!*

HEATBLAST APPEARS, BUT THERE'S SOMETHING DIFFERENT ABOUT HIM – THE NORMALLY HOT ALIEN HAS BEN'S COLD ...

YOU GUYS SHUT DOWN THE REACTOR. I'LL TAKE CARE OF BUGSY.

HEATBLAST THROWS HIMSELF AT CLANCY, BUT HE IS **SMACKED** BACK INTO THE WALL.

THAT'S IT. TIME TO TURN UP THE HEATBLAST ROUND HERE!

HEATBLAST AIMS A STREAM OF FLAME TO FRY CLANCY AND THE BUGS, BUT ALL HE CAN MANAGE IS A LITTLE PUFF OF ICY BREATH OUT OF HIS NOSE AS HE SNEEZES ...

MY COLD! IT'S FROZEN MY FLAMES!

GRANDPA MAX AND GWEN HAVE RUN OFF TO FIND THE CORE ACCESS ROOM. THEY FIND HORNETS' NESTS ALL OVER THE CORRIDOR'S WALLS AND CEILING.

UH, OH. REMEMBER THE OLD EXPRESSION 'MEAN AS A HORNET'?

MELTDOWN IN ... **FIVE** MINUTES ...

MAX SPOTS A FIRE EXTINGUISHER. HE HANDS THE NOZZLE TO GWEN AND THEN CRANKS THE WATER ON FULL. GWEN STRUGGLES TO STAY ON HER FEET AS SHE AIMS THE POWERFUL SPRAY AT THE HORNETS, BUT IT WORKS ...

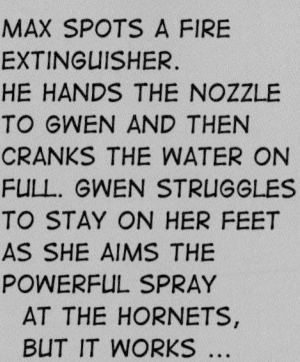

MEANWHILE, BACK IN THE MAIN CONTROL ROOM ...

THE CLANCY BUG MASS IS KICKING HEATBLAST'S BUTT AROUND THE CONTROL ROOM. THE ALIEN HERO TRIES TO FIGHT BACK.

OH MAN, MAYBE WE CAN TALK ABOUT THIS. HEY ...

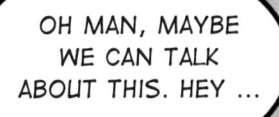

CHILLY HEATBLAST MAY NOT BE ABLE TO SHOOT FIRE, BUT HE CAN SHOOT *ICE!*

THE CLANCY-BUG MASS LUMBERS TOWARDS HEATBLAST AS THE HERO SHOOTS BLAST AFTER ICY BLAST AT THE VILLAIN ...

CLANCY STARTS FREEZING OVER. HE TRIES TO TAKE ONE LAST, DESPERATE SWIPE AT HEATBLAST, BUT HIS ARM IS FROZEN SOLID.

RESULT! HEATBLAST ADMIRES HIS GIANT ICE SCULPTURE. BUT THE VICTORY MOMENT IS SHORT AND SWEET ...

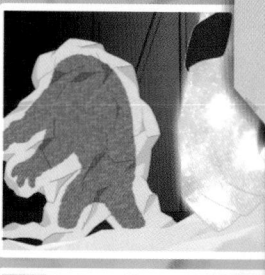

CORE TEMPERATURE CRITICAL. MELTDOWN IN ... **ONE** MINUTE ...

CORE MELTDOWN IN **TEN** ... **NINE** ... **EIGHT** ... **SEVEN** ... **SIX** ... **FIVE** ...

HEATBLAST HAS AN IDEA. HE SHOOTS MORE ICY STREAMS AT THE NUCLEAR REACTOR CORE. THE COOL DOWN SOON STARTS TO WORK AND THE CORE TEMPERATURE BEGINS TO DROP.

... FOUR ... THREE ... TWO ... CORE TEMPERATURE FALLING ... RETURNING TO BELOW CRITICAL LIMITS ...

AWESOME!

HEATBLAST HAS SAVED THE DAY!

BEN, GRANDPA MAX AND GWEN ARE SAFELY BACK IN THE RUSTBUCKET, HEADING AWAY FROM THE NUCLEAR PLANT.

THE BAD GUY'S ON ICE, THE REACTOR'S CHILLIN' ... AND I THINK THAT STEAM KNOCKED OUT THE LAST OF MY COLD.

GWEN SUDDENLY NOTICES A SINGLE COCKROACH EMERGING FROM ONE OF THE CRACKS IN THE RUSTBUCKET. BEFORE SHE CAN CRUSH IT, A HUGE RIVER OF CREEPY CRAWLIES POURS INSIDE ...

WE'VE GOT COMPANY. LOTS OF COMPANY!

MAX PULLS OVER TO THE SIDE OF THE ROAD. AS HE DOES, CLANCY LANDS ON THE RUSTBUCKET, CARRIED IN ON HIS CARPET OF INSECTS ...

WE DIDN'T APPRECIATE THAT COLD SHOULDER YOU GAVE US AT THE POWER PLANT.

BEN TRIES THE OMNITRIX, BUT IT DOESN'T WORK.

HE THINKS FAST. BEN GRABS THE JAR OF HIS SICKLY SWEET COLD REMEDY AND WAVES IT AROUND AT THE MASS OF BUGS. THE INSECTS SWARM TOWARDS THE JAR.

COME AND GET IT!

WHAT'S HAPPENING? *STOP!*

WITHOUT HIS BUG ARMY, CLANCY COWERS IN THE CORNER. GRANDPA MAX APPROACHES HIM AND DELIVERS A POWERFUL *PUNCH*, LAYING THE INSECT DUDE OUT COLD.

BEN TOSSES THE JAR OUT THE DOOR OF THE RUSTBUCKET. ALL THE INSECTS FOLLOW THE BAIT. THEY STREAM OVER A CLIFF AND DOWN TO THE OCEAN FAR, FAR BELOW!

"GOOD. THAT GUY WAS REALLY STARTING TO BUG ME," LAUGHS GWEN.